# Dusty's TALE

ISBN 978-1-63814-341-3 (Paperback)
ISBN 978-1-63814-343-7 (Hardcover)
ISBN 978-1-63814-342-0 (Digital)

Covenant Books, Inc.
11661 Hwy 707
Murrells Inlet, SC 29576
www.covenantbooks.com

# Dusty's TALE

## CAROL ERNST

Hi! My name is Dusty, and I am a Shih Tzu.

Most of the day I sit here on top of the couch. I must admit, it is kind of comfy. But I have a job to do. Cars and trucks pass my house, and it is my job to let them know I am here at work. A bark here. A bark there. But do they listen to me when I tell them they don't belong here?

People walk by our house every day, all day long. Yesterday a lady with an open umbrella walked by, and it wasn't even raining! I must admit it was hot. Maybe she thought her umbrella would give her shade and keep her cool. I barked at the front window to let her know I saw her. Then I ran to the side window and then finally the back window. She acted as if I wasn't even there!

My mom is special. She has only two legs! She stands taller than me and wears these funny things she calls clothes. Even though we speak different languages, we have learned to communicate. She knows when I want to eat. When I need to go out for a walk. She also knows when I want to play or take a nap. I cuddle next to her at night and lick her face to tell her I love her.

Mom is trying to teach me new things. I have learned the words *sit*, *dinner*, and *Daddy's home*. I pretend not to know what she means when she says "Come" or "Stay." I like to do what I want when I want. Sometimes Mom gets angry with me, but I love her anyway.

My dad has two legs too! He is taller than Mom. At night he sneaks into the kitchen and takes food out of the refrigerator. Sometimes he shares. Other times he goes into his room and closes the door! Does he think he deserves treats more than me?

Since I am still a puppy, I sometimes get bored. I want to try new things. One late afternoon while Dad was cooking dinner on the grill, I snuck out the door when he wasn't looking. Freedom! I ran so fast!

It was starting to rain, but I didn't care. For a while it felt good because it was a hot summer evening. Then, there was a bright flashing light and a loud crackling sound. A loud rumble followed and scared me something awful!

I was confused about where I was. It was getting dark and I was alone. I couldn't smell the normal smells from my walks with Mom and Dad. Everything looked so different! How would I find my way back home? Did they even know I was gone?

I kept looking around for something I knew. I sniffed the ground but found nothing that would tell me where I was. There were no cars, no trucks. I didn't see anyone walking around that I knew. Was I even near my house? Did I wander so far away that I was completely lost? Would I ever see my mom and dad again? Would they miss me?

It seemed as if hours had passed. I was confused. I needed my mom and dad. I had no water except for the puddles on the ground. I had no food. I was soaking wet! Would Mom and Dad even know me if I found my way home?

Suddenly, between the flashing lights, crackling sky, and rumbling noise, I heard my name. "Dusty! Dusty! Where are you?" It was my mom and dad! They were looking for me!

I began to smell something I knew! Steak! It smelled like steak! I ran toward their voices. And there they were! I was so happy to see them! My tail wagged! I licked their faces! I enjoyed a good steak dinner that night. I don't think I will ever run out on my own again!

# ABOUT THE AUTHOR

Carol Ernst has been married to her husband, Peter, for over forty years. Together they have three children. She is known as Mom to one daughter and two sons and their spouses. Also known as GiGi to her four grandchildren and CeCe to the many children she has cared for over the years, she always enjoyed making up stories to tell them. Carol credits God for her love of children and her ability to tell a tale.

CPSIA information can be obtained
at www.ICGtesting.com
Printed in the USA
LVHW071936150222
711184LV00007B/307

9 781638 143413